This is a Flash Fiction Duology, published by Lombosco Publications-Canada.

Date published: April 15, 2021

The book's front cover and inside illustrations were done by Nisansala Alwis from Sri Lanka.

The front cover design depicts pretty near the entrance to the Lazareto Village. Its left side shows the cemetery while its right side is a small but still operational domestic airport for light aircrafts. Lazareto is vastly arrayed with mountains, a sea, a cave, and two islets. Years ago, Lazareto had three ports where big ships docked to unload the bulk of gasoline for the consumption of the whole province of Mindoro.

Dedication

I dedicate this book to-

Ms. Theresa Jacobs,

a Canadian Author
who influences me to write speculative, horror or
mystery fiction,
and who always supports me in my creative writing
career.

This book is also dedicated to my future **"Little
Cherubims"**,
my sweethopes' children.

- Author Lucy Lombos

***

I dedicate this book of folktales to-

My grandparents, **Nicolas and Regina**;
And to all my relatives and residents of Lazareto.

- Author Daniel Enriquez

Foreword

By
Precious Joy Pacho,
A Filipino English Teacher

Childhood would not be complete if we did not hear thrilling stories from our grandparents or the old tales from the townspeople. From mythical creatures who might take you to their kingdom, mysterious disappearances in the field, to the night lurkers who are amused in tricking humans--- "Monsters in Lazareto" indeed have made your heart stopped as a kid. Still without a doubt, they teach us lessons that we can bring as we grow older.

Why should children read stories about monsters and other unimaginable creatures? It is natural for us to think that the children would have nightmares and always be scared when dark. Through the creative minds of both fantastic writers, Daniel and Lucy, this writing project can prove that allowing young readers to reach and read such kinds of folktales is salient for their growth and development.

Lazareto tales bring you to the Philippines' southern province and offers you a glimpse of the country's culture and its people. Despite being a horror flash fiction, children will find it fun! The thrilling stories are encompassed with lessons wrapped in a compelling way of storytelling by Daniel and Lucy.

Daniel is a co-author of the riveting Horror Short Story Tetralogy, "After Six o' Clock". Lucy is a notable writer of children's books and is also a strong advocate of Child Development and Family Literacy. I call her the *wordplay master* as she can write children's books in any genre that are always worth the read for all ages!

The real world is scary. Life is mysteriously an incomplete and a fragmentary knowledge sans the monsters and mythical creatures. Hence, this book is a good window for the young generation to prepare for life's risks and dangers. This book is also the right choice to acknowledge their sensational emotions, to be responsible for their actions, and to mold them to be brave and respond with resiliency to any frightening situations in life that they face.

To the readers, may this flash fiction duology take you on a wonderful and thrilling ride as we all become the brave characters in life that will not waver no matter how daunting the path is.

Introduction

It takes two to tango, as the saying goes. For this particular writing project, "it takes two to write". Daniel Enriquez, my brother and co-author in "After Six o' Clock Nightfall", and I put our heads together to come up with these flash fiction stories, with mystery as theme. Both of us are familiar with different interesting folktales, but we narrowed them down and focused on two that set in a place called Lazareto. At one point in our lives, this little village, located in Calapan City, Oriental Mindoro, the Southern part of the Philippines, was home to us. In that place during our youth, we were immersed in many colorful stories. We felt that we had to share those unheard folktales with the young readers and with the young-at-heart. "Kapre" was penned by Daniel, while "Bungisngis, the Laughing Monster" was written by yours truly.

As part of our culture, I could feel that these accounts, though somewhat folksy and homey, may bring new excitement to and appreciation from the students, teachers, parents, storytellers, and other readers.

The readers would find the micro-stories quite scary and mystifying at the beginning and would unfold to an amusing ending. For sure, they would resonate with you because of its morals, particularly in understanding human weaknesses and strengths. The not-so-scary narratives will give you a glimpse of our roots and how rich our literature is. We hope that these ingenious folktales would allow our readers to take pleasure in a mystical ride and enjoy the chance to savor some meaningful lessons in life.

Through this medium intended for child development and family literacy, Daniel and I would like to connect to the diverse population in our native land; hopefully, it can reach other countries in the world.

- Lucy Lombos
Author of Children's Books and other Multiple Genres,
Reading and Language Teacher,
Former Kabataang Barangay (Youth) Chairman in Lazareto and one of the Kabataang Barangay Board of Directors in Calapan City, Oriental Mindoro, Philippines

Daniel Enriquez and Lucy Lombos

Monsters in Lazareto

~Flash Fiction Duology for Children and Families~

Illustrated by Nisansala Alwis

Kapre

By Daniel Enriquez

"Vicente, Vicente, Vi...," a nearby voice called the name of a young Filipino. It blared at midnight. Often, it softened and faded away at its third, creepy call.

As a man of pure heart and conquering spirit, this Filipino guy was known in the village. He lived at the nipa house with stilts at its flooring in Lazareto, a small village in Calapan, Oriental Mindoro, Philippines. His home had 'silong', a semi-basement area of the typical nipa hut.

The voice pestered Vicente, who couldn't believe why him of all the village folks. Once he heard the voice, he couldn't sleep anymore because it sent shivers to his whole being. Much ado, he could strongly feel that the mysterious voice belonged to a monster.

"Whoever he is, what's his message to me?" Vicente wondered with fear.

Then, one cold midnight when the moon displayed its full brightness, the voice cried out again, "Vicente, Vicente, Vi...". It annoyed him, but he couldn't do anything. In fact, he trembled when that horrid voice called out his name.

Summer came. "Vicente, Vicente, Vi..."

Once more, he heard the voice that came from the direction of his window. He was fed up. Decided to settle this incident, he readied himself and looked out the window of his bedroom. With a clenched jaw and hurried steps, he went to the kitchen and returned to his bedroom. This time with bolo, a large single-edged knife, on his right hand, a rope on his shoulder, and a lamp on his left hand, he faced the invisible monster.

"Who are you?" Vicente, with tensed muscles, challenged the wicked creature which he would like to conquer and overthrow.

"Vicente, Vicente, Vi...".

"Oh, come on! Show yourself to me!" Vicente challenged the bedeviled creature. He would like to end this bothering hassle to him.

Kapre, an evil giant who dwells on the tree, appeared. The bulky, powerful creature smokes tobacco and draws human attention.

"I am Kapre!" the bony humanoid creature said.

"Kapre, what do you really want from me?" Vicente raised his shaky voice, all set to defeat the giant.

Kapre blew the thick tobacco smoke at Vicente.

"Don't fool me!" Vicente warned Kapre.

"I'm not fooling you!" Kapre, ghastly looking, replied with a rough tone.

"I did not do anything wrong against you. What do you really want from me?" Vicente insisted, keeping a firm hold of his weapons.

"Well, you did not really harm me. The truth is I can see you day in and day out. You are kind and hard working. Well, this is the day to relax a bit!" Kapre replied in a loud voice that only Vicente could hear.

"Don't go around the bush. Tell me at once," Vicente said with bravado.

"Easy! Now, go to your 'silong'," Kapre gave the initial instruction to Vicente.

Upon hearing this instruction, Vicente thought it might be a tricky danger that awaited him underneath the house.

"Why are you telling this command to me," Vicente asked, still gripping his bolo, rope and lamp.

"I'm not joking you!"

"Why me?"

"Because you have a good heart. I can see you're a true gentleman."

"Seriously?"

"Go out and find the golden hen with its priceless chicks below your house," Kapre instructed him further.

Confused but slightly sensing the sincerity of the Kapre, Vicente asked, "Then, what will I do once I found the golden hen and its chicks?"

"Follow them. Remember the spot where they exactly disappeared."

"Why? I don't understand?" Vicente asked and scratched his head.

Kapre continued, "Go to the exact location of their quick disappearance. Then, dig the pit right there. You will be rich, Vicente!"

Their conversations went long because Vicente was quite afraid, and Kapre smoked without interruption.

Determined to finish this encounter, overwhelmed though, Vicente pronounced, "I can do it!"

"You will be rich!" Kapre repeated and warned him, "Let this be a secret. No one should see you. Make it quick!"

Vicente hurried downstairs with his weapons and tools.

At the 'silong', he saw right before his eyes the golden hen and its chicks. They disappeared like magic. So, without reluctance, he dug the land and made the big pit. To his surprise, he saw a jar of gold.

"There you are!... This is unbelievable."

Then, the roosters began to crow.

When he was about to lift the jar of gold, his neighbor saw him and called out his name.

The neighbor exclaimed, "Hey, Vicente! What are you doing there?"

Startled that someone was awake, he replied, "Oh, I'm just cleaning here! No problem. Thanks!"

"Ah, ok! I thought you just need help!" his neighbor shouted.

Thereupon, the golden jar went to the innermost part of the pit and waned.

"This is strange!" Vicente said as he tried to pull it up. Alas, it slipped out of his hands. Then, it escaped from his sight.

He sat down, feeling anxious, yet he reflected, "If this is a genuine gold as a gift from the Creator of everything good, it will be wholeheartedly given to me. Ah, maybe this is only a horrific prank."

At once, Kapre hid after duping Vicente. Sometimes, he would only like to play tricks on humans.

Vicente remained silent and went on, "I believe that riches should be rightly earned. Ah, Kapre deceived me... I would never ever trust again anyone who came from the entire race of the king of darkness."

Since then, Kapre had never bothered Vicente anymore.

Vicente became free and was peaceful at sleep. Living a simple life, he continued to work hard and do good things for many people.

But one day outside his neighbor's house...

A cloud of tobacco smoke appeared from the top of the tree.

~The End~

Bungisngis

~The Laughing Monster~

By Lucy Lombos

On a cloudy day, two hunters started their adventure towards the seashore's farthest part where a cave was situated. They alerted themselves to the weird sounds around them.

"It's dangerous out there!" The folks had told them and advised them, "Be extra careful."

One ill-famed tale made the people cautious and frightened to go out hunting and sailing. They said that the loud and wild laughter of the real monster could be heard any time at the cave and at the seashore in a small hamlet named, Lazareto.

The monster's sound may seem cheerful at first, but listening with eager attention to it would give one the chills. Its roar invited fear of a specific threat. In Lazareto, it had become notorious since the ancient years when the great-great-grandfathers of the native storytellers existed.

Not so long...

"Ha, ha, ha, ha!" the monster laughed to attract the folks' awareness of its presence.

Obviously looking for its prey, this horrifying creature loved to distract people with its come-on laughter.

"Ha, ha, ha, ha!"... "Ha, ha, ha, ha!" A burst of joyous laughter was heard anew.

"Did you hear that? It is true then! The laughter could trick you. It does sound merry, but there is something demonic about it at the same time," Nicolas uttered, sensing a risk in the cave.

Later...

"Ha, ha, ha, ha!"

"Oh my God! What a hair-raising sound! I have not seen that monster, though. You?" Nicolas asked Victor.

"No, I haven't, too. And I want to keep it that way! The residents and even my family have said that it's terrifying," Victor, older than Nicolas, replied.

"What is its name?"

"It is called Bungisngis!"

"Bungisngis?" Nicolas at once asked.

"Yeah, Bungisngis, the laughing monster!" Victor prompted.

"Why? How...What does it look like?" Nicolas stammered and wondered. He couldn't imagine its features.

All of a sudden, the laughter could be heard again. "Ha, ha, ha, ha!" It felt like a deafening explosion inside the cave.

"Quick! Let's get out of here before it catches us," Victor burst out.

"Ok, let's go!" Nicolas agreed. They rushed to the cave's exit.

They were about to get out when they noticed a floating log hindering their way. It was huge and was covered with moss.

"Can you move the log just a bit to let us out?" Nicolas asked, "I will hold the torch."

"I will try," Victor said and tried, "It's heavy!"

"Ok, let me give you a hand," Nicolas offered and said," We don't want Bungisngis to see us!"

Victor looked around, trying to see a way to go out of the cave. Then, he saw a piece of driftwood.

"What shall we do?" Nicolas asked, feeling nervous.

"Together, we lift this briny-smelling log with this driftwood," Victor suggested. He seemed to be more focused and not panicky. But the two of them failed to lift the log.

Just in time, in silence, the creature showed up behind them.

Lo and behold, the wicked Bungisngis was real and alive! They could not imagine the fright they were feeling at that moment.

"Bungisngis looks like a ball," Nicolas expressed in a shocked tone.

"Be quiet. Let's not anger it. We have to go!" Victor hushed his partner. He helped Nicolas lift the log.

Meanwhile, the laughter of Bungisngis rang on and on. They finally had a good look at his face. A huge mouth and thick lips almost covered its entire face when laughing.

"Come on, let's give it one more try....ONE, TWO, THREE!" Victor shouted. Together they lifted the log with all their strength. After some time, they did it.

After the log was out of their way, like bullets, they escaped from the cave. Victor checked on his hunting tools, as well as his Polaroid instant camera.

As soon as the two hunters were out of the cave, they noticed that everything became quiet. Bungisngis have stopped with his crazy laughter. They recalled the words of the village folks.

The settlers said, "When that beastly creature becomes quiet, it signifies danger... time to eat its prey!"

As they went on their way away from the cave, they turned around and saw Bungisngis standing still, its face in full view. His monstrous entirety was clear. Victor was swift to grab his camera and wasted no time. He took a quick photo of the scary freak.

"Whew, that was so close!" Nicolas sighed, catching his breath when they were already out, and proceeded to Punta, a high land point in Lazareto.

"I captured him!" Victor remarked in a winning tone, showing the photo from his camera.

"You're incredibly brave!" Nicolas commented with a jumpy spirit. He tapped Victor's right shoulder and smiled at him, "Now, we can show other people what Bungisngis really looks like!"

They moved their heads closer to gape at the camera screen. Their excitement faded. The picture surprised them. The parts of the cave looked clear, as well as the waters. But on the spot where Bungisngis stood looked nothing like the monster. There was just a hazy shadow.

Then, from the rocky promontory, overlooking the lowland and the seashore, Nicolas and Victor stood bewildered and frustrated. They stared at the cave with unanswered questions. They saw pieces of driftwood floating near the cave's mouth. Piles of wood might have given Bungisngis a hard time chasing them.

"Ha, ha, ha, ha!"

On other days, people would claim that they could still hear Bungisngis' laughter. It would ring loud and scary.

It would beckon a summoned hunter, a fisherman, or a sailor.

"Hey, could Bungisngis be a friend to a mermaid?" Nicolas asked.

"Perhaps! Mermaids are said to have a certain laugh that charms the town folks as well," Victor answered.

"What if Bungisngis disguises as a mermaid?" Nicolas asked.

"I would make sure to take about twenty photos!" Victor said. Then, he roared, "Ha, ha ha ha!"

Nicolas gazed open-mouthed at him as his friend sounded exactly like Bungisngis.

~The End~

The Author of "Kapre"

Daniel D. Enriquez was born and raised in the Philippines. He graduated with Honors in BS Marine Biology, Batch 1986 from a prestigious University of San Carlos, Cebu City, Philippines.

For more than three decades until now, he works at the private company as an Administrator. He is based in Puerto Galera, Oriental Mindoro, with his wife and two sons. With that job and other opportunities, he practices his profession. He participates in the Tourism, Literacy, and Conservation of his town. Alongside, he serves Puerto Galera (PG) by being a Municipal Councilor for 12 years (elected for 4 terms), holding the chairmanship of the Committee on Environment & Agriculture.

In 2021, he became the Philippine Coast Guard Auxiliary with the rank of Lieutenant.

Moreover, his list of involvement goes on. He is a Board of Director of PG Most Beautiful Bays in the World, Inc., Board Member of PG Coastal Resources & Environmental Management Board, Member of the PG Tourism Council, and Municipal Advisory Council. To note, he wrote forty-seven environmental ordinances, aside from municipal resolutions and non-environmental ordinances for his hometown.

As to his educational achievements and other accolades, he obtained awards such as Valedictorian in Elementary and in High School at the Puerto Galera Academy, and University Cum Laude, as mentioned above. Regarding his contributions and services to the nation through politics and good governance, he was a "3 Termer-Awardee" of the Philippine Councilor's League.

Last year, during the pandemic's peak (2020), he wrote a horror short story. He co-authored it in "After Six o' Clock Nightfall". As a man of few words but of so many smart ideas and a great passion for Marine Ecosystem, he edited the children's environmental book, "The Tale of Bill, the Butterflyfish," written by his youngest son, Dexter Jethro C. Enriquez.

The Author of "Bungisngis, the Laughing Monster"

Hi! **Lucy E. Lombos** is the author of one of the folktales in this book.
Each letter of her first name has meaning.

L- Light. Yes, that's right, the bubbly light of the family! She is a loving daughter and sister, a wife, a mom of three sweethopes, a jolly friend and a brilliant teacher. She always asks the Holy Spirit to enlighten her mind, to inspire her and guide her all the time. Praise God! Modesty aside, she graduated with Honours- Valedictorian in Elementary, Silver Medallist with General Excellence Award in High School and Cum Laude in College. In De La Salle University, Taft, Manila, she pursued her graduate studies; and completed the academic units at the University of the Philippines where she specialized in Language and Literacy. She further enhanced her English proficiency skills by enrolling in a TESOL (Teaching English to Speakers of Other Languages) with Practicum Course in Vancouver, British Columbia, Canada.

U- Understanding. She has a substantial and deep understanding of her profession. She undertakes teaching the English fundamental skills, and these are – Speaking, Reading, Writing and Listening. She founded Lombosco Academy in the Philippines in 2000 and she remains the Academy Directress, and the Editor-In-Chief of its Newsletter.

C- Children. They are the subject of her craft. She studied courses about Writing for Children, Writing a Life Story, and Writing Young Adult Novel in Canada. She also earned a Diploma in Child Psychology in USA. In Spring time of 2020, she enrolled in Child Protection: Children's Rights in Theory and Practice at the Harvard University edX.

Y- Young. She is always young at heart. She would like to learn more. She never stops resting on her laurels. She enjoys blogging and contributing articles for different media. Further, she is a member of ILA- International Literacy Association and Society of Children's Book Writers and Illustrators.

*N.B. *In the Philippines, Lucy taught at Puerto Galera Academy after her College Graduation; later, she became the Principal at Prince of Peace Montessori. *Through her authored books, in 2017, Puerto Galera's Sangguniang Bayan gave her an Official Recognition for promoting tourism in that province; In October 2019, another Special Recognition was awarded to her by the Puerto Galera Tourism Council. *She always gives and donates FREE Books, and she says, "It's my wish that my books would find their way to all young readers' hands and hearts."*

*** Other Published Books by Lucy Lombos***

Ang Tinago Kong Piso/The Peso-Coin I Kept

The Class Lady Bug

The Star of the Sea: A Boat Ride

Happiness 365 and ¼ Days (a biography)

'Ter and Ter', the Turtle and the Eagle

The Joys of Junior

Swanie's Bag

Rose of Calapan (a novel)

Bono (an early chapter book)

Three Fables, Part 1: Keys to Change the Heart,

Three Fables, Part 2: Sparks to Brighten one's Purpose in Life

Pinky Oinky

Gracie and Dots

After Six o' Clock Nightfall

Noshi

One Drop, Two Drops and Much More

Ellie-Phant and Mon-Keysha

*** Her upcoming books are- ***

Ely's Gift

Cotton and Nibbles

Beary G

and

The Seed

SPECIAL REQUEST

To all those who bought and read this book-

If you loved this Flash Fiction Duology and have a minute to spare, the authors would really appreciate a short review from you to be posted on the site where you bought or read the book. Your help in spreading kind words is a great succor to other readers, especially to the young children from different parts of the world.

GREAT THANKS!

Acknowledgment

We would like to express our deep gratitude to the following people for giving us the big support which we humbly needed in writing this book –

Umberto L. Lombos for publishing this book;

Annie Datu-Enriquez and Theresa Jacobs for editing the manuscript;

Precious Joy Pacho for the Foreword,

Theresa Jacobs, Kate Hampton, Sherman M., and James Belleza,

for writing the wonderful blurbs for this flash fiction duology,

and to our families for giving us the moral support.

We are truly happy and grateful to you all.

Without your generous help, this book may not have been possible.